PLAY-ALONG BLUES WITH A LIVE BAND!

PLAY-ALONG BLUES
WITH A LIVE BAND!

WISE PUBLICATIONS

part of The Music Sales Group

London / New York / Paris / Sydney / Copenhagen / Berlin / Madrid / Tokyo

Published by
WISE PUBLICATIONS
14-15 Berners Street, London W1T 3LJ, UK.

Exclusive Distributors:
MUSIC SALES LIMITED
Distribution Centre, Newmarket Road, Bury St Edmunds, Suffolk IP33 3YB, UK.
MUSIC SALES PTY LIMITED
20 Resolution Drive, Caringbah, NSW 2229, Australia.

Order No. AM991969
ISBN 978-1-84772-294-2
This book © Copyright 2008 Wise Publications, a division of Music Sales Limited.

Compiled by Nick Crispin
Edited by Fiona Bolton
Music arranged by Paul Honey
Music processed by Paul Ewers Music Design
Song Background Notes by Michael Heatley
Cover design by Adela Casacuberta
Text photographs courtesy LFI
Printed in the EU

CD recorded, mixed and mastered by Jonas Persson
Alto Saxophone: John Whelan
Keyboard: Paul Honey
Guitar: Arthur Dick
Bass: Don Richardson
Drums: Chris Baron

Song Background Notes

Baby What You Want Me To Do?
Jimmy Reed

Born Mathis James Reed in Dunleith, Mississippi in 1925, Jimmy hit the Chicago blues scene with childhood friend Eddie Taylor, who taught him guitar; he also played harmonica and sang. Reed recorded for Vee-Jay Records from 1953, scoring seven Top 10 R&B hits, making him one of the most consistently popular Chicago bluesmen. Elvis Presley, Van Morrison, The Everly Brothers and Neil Young are among those to have covered 'Baby What You Want Me To Do?', which became his second highest-charting single in the US pop chart in 1960.

Call It Stormy Monday (But Tuesday Is Just As Bad)
T-Bone Walker

Aaron 'T-Bone' Walker titled his song to avoid confusion with 'Stormy Monday Blues', a No. 1 R&B hit recorded in 1942 by Earl Hines and Billy Eckstine. The new song reached No. 5 on the R&B charts in 1948 and encouraged B. B. King to begin playing electric guitar. Walker re-recorded the song on his 1959 Atlantic album *T-Bone Blues* and it has since been covered by innumerable blues and rock artists, most notably the Allman Brothers Band. A 1988 movie, *Stormy Monday*, took its name from the song and featured B. B. King's performance over the credits.

Hi-Heel Sneakers
Tommy Tucker

Ohio-born singer-keyboardist Robert Higginbotham changed his name to Tommy Tucker and found fame in 1964 with this self-penned R&B classic that crossed over to the US pop Top 20 on Chess Records' subsidiary Checker label. The version issued was the original demo recording. Since then everybody from Elvis through The Beatles to Tom Jones has covered his first and greatest three minutes. When his follow-up, the similar 'Long Tall Shorty', failed to scale the charts, Tucker retired from music to become an estate agent!

I'd Rather Go Blind
Etta James

Recorded and released by Etta James in 1967, this was a major UK hit for British blues band Chicken Shack a year later when sung by Christine Perfect, later Christine McVie of Fleetwood Mac. Others to have covered it since include Rod Stewart, B.B. King and Paul Weller. Etta James claims to have co-written the song with Ellington Jordan but, for tax reasons, gave her partner, Billy Foster, the credit. Her version was released as the B-side of the single 'Tell Mama', and was included by film-maker Martin Scorsese in his acclaimed 2003 documentary series on the blues.

The Lady Sings The Blues
Billie Holiday

Tragic lives don't come any more tear-jerking than that of Billie Holiday, and 'The Lady Sings The Blues' was chosen to title her 1956 autobiography. It was also the name of the biopic of her life made by Motown's Berry Gordy in 1972 and starring Diana Ross in the title role. The album of the same name went to No.1 in the US, Ross's only solo chart-topper, though 'The Lady Sings The Blues' itself was scarcely more than a minute long. Holiday's nickname was Lady Day, hence the title of the song which she wrote with Herbie Nichols.

Need Your Love So Bad
Fleetwood Mac

Fleetwood Mac took a song by jailed bluesman Little Willie John and produced not only the definitive version, but a 1968 UK hit available on the *Pious Bird Of Good Omen* album. Band founder, singer and guitarist Peter Green had first heard the original while working with John Mayall's Bluesbreakers; Mayall played him B.B. King's version, inspiring Green to employ Mickey Baker of Mickey and Sylvia 'Love Is Strange' fame to orchestrate the now-customary ear-catching backing strings.

Please Send Me Someone To Love
Percy Mayfield

This R&B chart-topping blues ballad was written and recorded by Percy Mayfield for Specialty Records in 1950. It was a prayer-like lyric that not only covered affairs of the heart but also, rarely for the time, included a demand for racial tolerance long before (the unrelated) Curtis Mayfield and Marvin Gaye made such things popular. Jeff Buckley, Slade and B. B. King are among its coverers. Mayfield, who is best known for writing Ray Charles' No.1 'Hit The Road, Jack', was facially disfigured in a car crash two years after this recording.

Sweet Home Chicago
Robert Johnson

Known by most as a showstopper of the *Blues Brothers* movie, this song was one of just 29 recordings made by legendary bluesman Robert Johnson before his mysterious death in 1938. His version emerged as a 78rpm disc on the Vocalion record label in 1936, the year it was recorded in San Antonio, Texas (many miles from Chicago), but like most 'race records' of the time was not a major seller. It has since become a blues standard, played by everyone from Buddy Guy (Louisiana-born but an adopted son of Chicago) to Britain's Eric Clapton, who rates Johnson as 'the most important blues musician that ever lived'.

Robert Johnson

Billie Holiday

The Thrill Is Gone
B. B. King

B. B. King's first success outside the blues market was his 1969 recording of 'The Thrill Is Gone'. He had heard blues pianist/composer Roy Hawkins perform 'and I thought it was a good idea so I re-wrote the tune. The lines you hear are the ones that I wrote. I carried it around with me for eight years but we'd never hit it like I wanted it. But that night everything seemed to be just right.' The song also benefited from a string arrangement from Bert DeCoteaux. King's version became a hit on both pop and R&B charts while he promoted it as opening act on The Rolling Stones' American tour.

Wang Dang Doodle
Koko Taylor

Koko Taylor was one of the few females signed by legendary blues label Chess Records. 'Wang Dang Doodle' had been written by the legendary Willie Dixon for Howlin' Wolf several years before her version made the Top 5 of the R&B charts in 1966. Wolf did not like it, calling it a 'levee camp' song, but Koko (real name Cora Walton) made it hers alone. Legend has it Dixon approached Taylor after a feisty performance with Howlin' Wolf's band. He told her, 'My God, I never heard a woman sing the blues like you. That's what the world needs today, a woman with a voice like yours.' A million-selling single was the result.

Fleetwood Mac

B. B. King

9

FREE bonus material

Download band scores and parts to your computer.

Visit www.hybridpublications.com

Registration is free and easy.

Your registration code is: FB545

Call It Stormy Monday
(But Tuesday Is Just As Bad)

Words & Music by T-Bone Walker

Demo track: Track 02
Backing track: Track 12

Baby What You Want Me To Do?

Words & Music by Jimmy Reed

Demo track: Track 03
Backing track: Track 13

Moderate swing feel

Hi-Heel Sneakers

Words & Music by Robert Higgenbotham

Demo track: Track 04
Backing track: Track 14

I'd Rather Go Blind

Words & Music by Ellington Jordan & Billy Foster

Demo track: Track 05
Backing track: Track 15

Slowly ♩ = 60

The Lady Sings The Blues

Words by Billie Holiday
Music by Herbie Nichols

Demo track: Track 06
Backing track: Track 16

Need Your Love So Bad

Words & Music by Mertis John Jr.

Demo track: Track 07
Backing track: Track 17

Steadily

24

cresc.

27

4

30

mf

33

36

39

41

rall.

45

dim.

21

Please Send Me Someone To Love

Words & Music by Percy Mayfield

Demo track: Track 08
Backing track: Track 18

Sweet Home Chicago

Words & Music by Robert Johnson

Demo track: Track 09
Backing track: Track 19

The Thrill Is Gone

Words & Music by Roy Hawkins & Rick Darnell

Demo track: Track 10
Backing track: Track 20

Moderately ♩ = 90

rall.

Wang Dang Doodle

Words & Music by Willie Dixon

Demo track: Track 11
Backing track: Track 21

Also available...

PLAY-ALONG Jazz WITH A JAZZ JAZZ TRIO

PLAY-ALONG Jazz WITH A JAZZ TRIO — alto sax
Ten classic jazz standards specially arranged for Alto Saxophone in melody line arrangements with demo and backing tracks on CD featuring a live band!

PLAY-ALONG Jazz WITH A JAZZ TRIO — trombone
Ten classic jazz standards specially arranged for Trombone in melody line arrangements with demo and backing tracks on CD featuring a live band!
Includes audio CD and free internet downloads!

PLAY-ALONG Jazz WITH A JAZZ TRIO — flute
Ten classic jazz standards specially arranged for Flute in melody line arrangements with demo and backing tracks on CD featuring a live band!

PLAY-ALONG Jazz WITH A JAZZ TRIO — trumpet
Ten classic jazz standards specially arranged for Trumpet in melody line arrangements with demo and backing tracks on CD featuring a live band!
Includes audio CD and free internet downloads!

PLAY-ALONG Jazz WITH A JAZZ TRIO — clarinet
Ten classic jazz standards specially arranged for Clarinet in melody line arrangements with demo and backing tracks on CD featuring a live band!
Includes audio CD and free internet downloads!

Birdland *Weather Report*
Cantaloupe Island *Herbie Hancock*
Desafinado (Slightly Out Of Tune) *Antonio Carlos Jobim*
Fly Me To The Moon (In Other Words) *Julie London*
Let's Get Lost *Chet Baker*
So What *Miles Davis*
Straight No Chaser *Thelonious Monk*
Take Five *Dave Brubeck*
Take The 'A' Train *Duke Ellington*
When The Saints Go Marching In *Louis Armstrong*

Each edition contains music in melody line arrangements, a CD with professional 'soundalike' performances and backing tracks, plus free internet downloads.

JAZZ ORDER NUMBERS...
Alto Saxophone *AM991881*
Clarinet *AM991870*
Flute *AM991859*
Trombone *AM992904*
Trumpet *AM991892*

Each edition contains music in melody line arrangements, a CD with professional 'soundalike' performances and backing tracks, plus free internet downloads.

PLAY-ALONG SOUL
WITH A LIVE BAND!

Cry To Me *Solomon Burke*
I Get The Sweetest Feeling *Jackie Wilson*
I Got You (I Feel Good) *James Brown*
In The Midnight Hour *Wilson Pickett*
Knock On Wood *Eddie Floyd*
Son Of A Preacher Man *Dusty Springfield*
Soul Man *Sam & Dave*
Stand By Me *Ben E. King*
Tired Of Being Alone *Al Green*
Try A Little Tenderness *Otis Redding*

SOUL ORDER NUMBERS...
Alto Saxophone *AM991925*
Clarinet *AM991914*
Flute *AM991903*
Trombone *AM992893*
Trumpet *AM991936*

ALL TITLES ARE AVAILABLE FROM YOUR LOCAL MUSIC RETAILER.
IN CASE OF DIFFICULTY, CONTACT THE MARKETING DEPARTMENT,
MUSIC SALES LIMITED, NEWMARKET ROAD, BURY ST EDMUNDS, SUFFOLK IP33 3YB, UK

marketing@musicsales.co.uk

CD Track Listing

1 Tuning Note

DEMONSTRATION TRACKS

2 Call It Stormy Monday (But Tuesday Is Just As Bad) (Walker) Burlington Music Company Limited.

3 Baby What You Want Me To Do? (Reed) Tristan Music Limited.

4 Hi-Heel Sneakers (Higgenbotham) Jewel Music Publishing Company Limited.

5 I'd Rather Go Blind (Jordan/Foster) Jewel Music Publishing Company Limited.

6 The Lady Sings The Blues (Holiday/Nichols) Universal/MCA Music Limited.

7 Need Your Love So Bad (John Jr.) Lark Music Limited.

8 Please Send Me Someone To Love (Mayfield) Sony/ATV Music Publishing (UK) Limited.

9 Sweet Home Chicago (Johnson) Interstate Music Limited/Paul Rodriguez Music Limited.

10 The Thrill Is Gone (Hawkins/Darnell) BMG Music Publishing Limited.

11 Wang Dang Doodle (Dixon) Bug Music Limited/Jewel Music Publishing Company Limited.

BACKING TRACKS

12 Call It Stormy Monday (But Tuesday Is Just As Bad)

13 Baby What You Want Me To Do?

14 Hi-Heel Sneakers

15 I'd Rather Go Blind

16 The Lady Sings The Blues

17 Need Your Love So Bad

18 Please Send Me Someone To Love

19 Sweet Home Chicago

20 The Thrill Is Gone

21 Wang Dang Doodle

To remove your CD from the plastic sleeve,
Lift the small lip to break the perforations.
Replace the disc after use for convenient storage.